PANCAKES

FOR

BREAKFAST

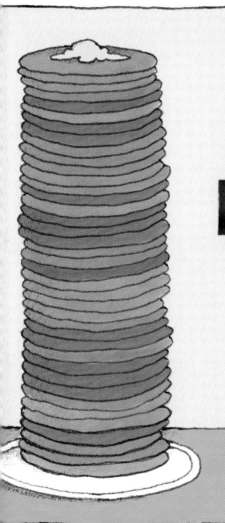

PANCAKES
FOR
BREAKFAST

BY

TOMIE DEPAOLA

HARCOURT, INC.

Orlando Austin New York San Diego Toronto London

FOR BETTY CAVE ♡

For information about permission to reproduce selections from this book, please write
Permissions, Houghton Mifflin Harcourt Publishing Company 215 Park Avenue South
NY NY 10003.

www.hmhbooks.com

Voyager Books is a registered trademark of Harcourt, Inc.

LIBRARY OF CONGRESS CATALOGING-IN-PUBLICATION DATA
dePaola, Thomas Anthony.
Pancakes for breakfast.
Summary: A little old lady's attempts to have
pancakes for breakfast are hindered by a scarcity
of supplies and participation of her pets.
[1. Stories without words.]   I. Title.
PZ7.D439PAN   77-15523
ISBN-13: 978-0-15-259455-8   ISBN-10: 0-15-259455-8
ISBN-13: 978-0-15-670768-8 pb   ISBN-10: 0-15-670768-3 pb

SCP   50 49 48 47 46 45 44 43 42
4500376881

Manufactured in China